Amazing Grace

Mary Hoffman

Illustrated by
Caroline Binch

FRANCES LINCOLN

Grace was a girl who loved stories.

   She didn't mind if they were read to her or told to her or made up in her own head. She didn't care if they were from books or on TV or in films or on the video or out of Nana's long memory. Grace just loved stories.

   And after she had heard them, or sometimes while they were still going on, Grace would act them out. And she always gave herself the most exciting part.

Grace went into battle as Joan of Arc . . .

and wove a wicked web as Anansi the spiderman.

She hid inside the wooden horse at the gates of Troy . . .

she crossed the Alps with Hannibal and a hundred
elephants . . .

she sailed the seven seas
with a peg-leg
and a parrot.

She was Hiawatha, sitting by the shining Big-Sea-Water

and Mowgli in the back garden jungle.

But most of all Grace loved to act pantomimes. She liked to be Dick Whittington turning to hear the bells of London Town or Aladdin rubbing the magic lamp. The best characters in pantomimes were boys, but Grace played them anyway.

When there was no-one else around, Grace played all the parts herself. She was a cast of thousands. Paw-Paw the cat usually helped out.

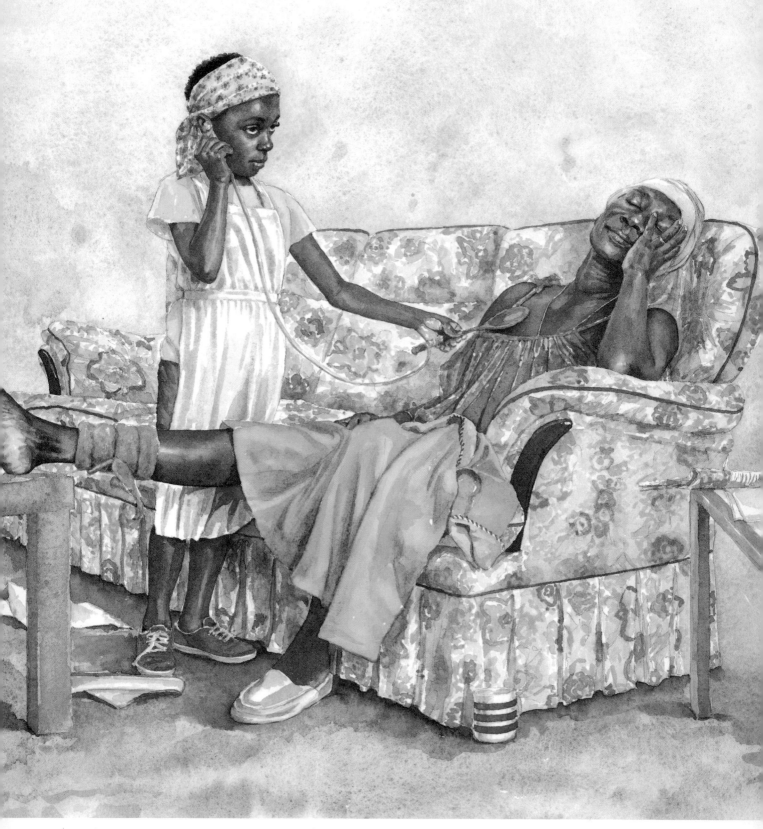

And sometimes she could persuade Ma and Nana
to join in, when they weren't too busy. Then she
was Doctor Grace and their lives were in her hands.

One day at school her teacher said they were going to do the play of *Peter Pan*. Grace put up her hand to be . . . Peter Pan.

"You can't be called Peter," said Raj. "That's a boy's name."

But Grace kept her hand up.

"You can't be Peter Pan," whispered Natalie. "He wasn't black." But Grace kept her hand up.

"All right," said the teacher. "Lots of you want to be Peter Pan, so we'll have to have auditions. We'll choose the parts next Monday."

When Grace got home, she
seemed rather sad.
   "What's the matter?"
asked Ma.
   "Raj said I couldn't be
Peter Pan because I'm a girl."
   "That just shows all Raj
knows about it," said Ma.
"Peter Pan is *always* a girl!"

Grace cheered up, then later she remembered
something else. "Natalie says I can't be Peter Pan
because I'm black," she said.

Ma started to get angry but Nana stopped her.

"It seems that Natalie is another one who don't
know nothing," she said. "You can be anything
you want, Grace, if you put your mind to it."

ROSALIE WILKINS in ROMEO & JULIET

ROMEO AND JULIET

ROSALI WILKINS

STUNNING NEW

Next day was Saturday and Nana told Grace they were going out. In the afternoon they caught a bus and a train into town. Nana took Grace to a grand theatre. Outside it said, "ROSALIE WILKINS in ROMEO AND JULIET" in beautiful sparkling lights.

"Are we going to the ballet, Nana?" asked Grace.

"We are, Honey, but I want you to look at these pictures first."

Nana showed Grace some photographs of a beautiful young girl dancer in a tutu. "STUNNING NEW JULIET!" it said on one of them.

"That one is little Rosalie from back home in
Trinidad," said Nana. "Her Granny and me, we
grew up together on the island. She's always asking
me do I want tickets to see her little girl dance – so
this time I said yes."

After the ballet, Grace played the part of Juliet,
dancing around her room in her imaginary tutu.
"I can be anything I want," she thought. "I can
even be Peter Pan."

On Monday they had the auditions. Their teacher let the class vote on the parts. Raj was chosen to play Captain Hook. Natalie was going to be Wendy.

Then they had to choose Peter Pan.

Grace knew exactly what to do – and all the words to say. It was a part she had often played at home. All the children voted for her.

"You were great," said Natalie.

The play was a great success and Grace was an amazing Peter Pan.

After it was all over, she said, "I feel as if I could fly all the way home!"

"You probably could," said Ma.

"Yes," said Nana. "If Grace put her mind to it – she can do anything she want."

For Buchi Emecheta *M.H.*
For Joe *C.B.*

Text copyright © Mary Hoffman 1991
Illustrations copyright © Caroline Binch 1991

First published in Great Britain in 1991 by
Frances Lincoln Limited, 4 Torriano Mews
Torriano Avenue, London NW5 2RZ

British Library Cataloguing in Publication Data
Hoffman, Mary *1945–*
Amazing grace.
I. Title   II. Binch, Caroline
823.914 [J]

ISBN 0-7112-0670-8 hardback
ISBN 0-7112-0699-6 paperback

Printed and bound in Hong Kong

9 11 13 15 14 12 10

HOFFMAN, M.
AMAZING GRACE   PICTURE BOOK

Cumbria

COUNTY COUNCIL

CUMBRIA HERITAGE SERVICES
LIBRARIES

This book is due to be returned on or before the last date above. It
may be renewed by personal application, post or telephone, if not in
demand.

C.L.18